LARGER  THAN LIFE

LARGER THAN LIFE

A novelization by J.J. Gardner
Based on the screenplay by Roy Blount, Jr.
and the story by Pen Densham and Gary Williams

SCHOLASTIC INC.
New York Toronto London Auckland Sydney

ISBN 0-590-95728-7

12 11 10 9 8 7 6 5 4 3 2 1   6 7 8 9/9 0 1/0
                                           40

Printed in the U.S.A.
First Scholastic printing, September 1996

LARGER THAN LIFE

1

Jack Corcoran stood backstage and nervously muttered to himself. "Beed'n, beed'n, beed'n," he said, trying to warm up his voice. "Over the lips, the teeth, the tongue. Beed'n, beed'n, beed . . ."

Jack could barely hear the audience on the other side of the curtain. They were sitting at their tables in the banquet hall quietly eating their dinners and listening to their company's event coordinator.

"This year has not been an easy one for the American Motion Upholstery industry," Jack heard the event coordinator say. "We must remind ourselves, as we listen to our guest speaker's inspiring words . . ."

Inspiring speaker, that's me. Jack laughed to himself as he limbered up by doing a few jumping jacks. He felt he could use some inspiration himself. The only thing his last motivational speech accomplished was to put the entire United Valve

Workers Company of Idaho to sleep. If that should happen here he could very well end up having to find something else to do for a living.

Just then the event coordinator appeared in the wings. "These people need something," he told Jack. "Their spirit is low. You're going to give them something, right?"

Jack gave the event coordinator a thumbs-up, trying to express confidence.

"One thing," the coordinator told Jack firmly. "And I cannot emphasize this enough: No jokes about the magic button!"

"What's a magic button?" asked Jack. He wasn't even sure what Motion Upholstery was. Then he remembered: It had something to do with reclining chairs. And the magic button? Oh, yeah. It didn't work. It was supposed to adjust your chair at the wave of a hand. Instead it flung you out of it like an ejector seat.

Jack's nervous thoughts were interrupted by a series of electronic beeps from inside his pocket. He reached in and pulled out his cellular phone.

"Hello?" he asked. "Mom? Yes, yes, I'll be there on time. I have to be on time for my introduction now. And please don't call during my speech."

No sooner had he put the phone back into his pocket than he heard the event coordinator begin to introduce him from the other side of the curtain:

". . . author of the book *Get Over It . . .*" went the introduction. "A rising star in the field of personal motivation . . . I'm sure you'll be glad you got to know . . . *Jack Cochran!*"

Corcoran, Jack thought, upset as he stepped out to the podium. Then he quickly took his own motivational advice and got over it.

A strong silence greeted Jack as he stood on the banquet hall stage. The room was filled with men and women. And all of them had the same expressions on their faces: They were bored.

"Before I was born my father died saving some other kid from drowning," began Jack. "Do you know how I felt about that, growing up? I resented it. It was years before I began to — *get over it!*"

Jack was trying to be enthusiastic, but the audience continued to look bored. Jack decided not to let that stop him. It was his job to get this audience excited.

"You wanna know what happened when I finally did *get over it?*" he asked buoyantly. "I found out some things! Neat things! About me! That I liked! That I wanted to share with other people who maybe didn't know neat things about themselves. People like you . . ."

Jack moved to a blackboard that had been set up behind him. He picked up a piece of chalk and drew a big *C*.

"When we're our negatives," he told the audience, "we're always saying '*See* I woulda, *see* I coulda.'"

He glanced out at the audience. They looked perplexed. Then he drew a huge *I* over the *C*.

"But when we *get over* our negatives," he added, "we say, '*I see!*'"

Jack looked out at the audience. Their expressions were still blank. Either he was bombing or the audience was having a hard time getting over it.

Thinking quickly, Jack grabbed a microphone. Then he energetically leaped off the stage and walked directly over to a table where a bespectacled man was nodding off.

"Sir, you weren't motivated," he said, rousing the man from his snooze. "I don't get that. We're basically the same person except I've got two eyes and you have four. Between us that's six. That's an extra eye each. Can you imagine what six eyes can accomplish together?"

Next Jack stepped over to a table where a man was making a stack out of some sugar cubes.

"Look at this guy," Jack said to the audience. "He's so bored he built a pyramid out of sugar. Okay, I'm gonna build a pyramid. Who's the biggest guy in this industry?"

Several people pointed to a man sitting a few tables away. Jack walked over to the man and pulled him from his chair.

"Okay, everyone down on their knees," he ordered. "C'mon, all fours, please, I mean it!" Without warning Jack organized several people into a human pyramid and placed the man at the top.

Now everyone in the audience was laughing hysterically. Everyone, that was, except the event coordinator. Jack noticed the dour-looking man eyeing him from the side of the stage.

"Uh-oh," he muttered. "Time to get back to business." And with that Jack pulled the big guy off the others and sent the human pyramid into a tumble. Encouraged by the audience's enthusiastic applause, he returned to the stage.

But no sooner had Jack resumed his motivational lecture than the audience began to look bored again. He tried his best to motivate them. He drew diagrams on the blackboard and told stories. He even gave examples from his own life. In the end nothing seemed to work. And when his speech was over there was hardly any applause at all.

"Jack Cochran, ladies and gentlemen," the events coordinator said, again getting Jack's last name wrong. "Are there any questions?"

"Whattaya think about the magic button?" someone shouted out to Jack. Jack saw the event coordinator cringe at the question.

"I wish I had the expertise to comment, there," said Jack, thinking quickly. "But, my friend, my business is motivation. You folks are . . ." he paused, momentarily forgetting the company's name. Then he remembered: "You folks are Motion Upholstery!"

The audience applauded.

Well, Jack thought as he walked off stage. *At least I got one thing right.*

2

Jack sat in the back of the taxicab and watched the sun set behind the Manhattan skyline as he crossed the bridge into Brooklyn. He was tired. He was also disappointed. He had failed to get the Motion Upholstery people motivated and it bothered him. That wasn't good for business. The only way to make it in the motivational speaking business was by getting good word of mouth. Between today's results and that last job in Idaho Jack was worried that companies would stop hiring him. He would have to talk to Walter, his agent, about that later, and he made a mental note to do so.

After a while the taxi pulled up in front of his mother's brownstone apartment building. Jack paid the driver and got out, house keys and *Get Over It* motivational posters in hand. As he climbed the steps to his mother's apartment he began to feel slightly better. His mother and Celeste, his fiancée, were inside waiting for him.

By now they had probably finished all the preparations for the engagement party.

Jack was looking forward to the party and to seeing Celeste. She was good for him. He was glad he was going to marry her. Tonight he wanted just to relax and forget about his worries.

"Change out of your suit, sweetheart," Jack's mother, Vera, told him as he entered the apartment. She was an attractive woman in her early sixties. She kissed him on the cheek and placed a tray of party hors d'oeuvres on the table. Jack had been right. The apartment was completely ready for the party. And he could smell the delicious odor of food cooking in the kitchen.

Just behind his mother Jack saw a young woman approach. It was Celeste. He gave her a quick hello kiss.

"So how did it go?" asked Celeste.

"Great!" Jack said, lying about how well his speech had gone. "It took a while, but —"

"You didn't deviate from your speech, did you?" asked Jack's mom.

"No," Jack said, lying again. "Well, maybe just a little . . ."

"Oh," said Jack's mom with just a tinge of disappointment in her voice. Then she said to Celeste, "Walter says the organizers hate it when the crowd has *too* good a time."

"I guess they could hire a performer for that," Celeste agreed.

"Walter's not coming tonight, is he?" asked Jack.

"He'd be crushed if we didn't invite him to our engagement party," said Celeste insistently.

Jack rolled his eyes. He wasn't in the mood to see his young agent. It would only serve to remind him of the fiasco earlier that evening. But before long Jack had changed his clothes and the guests began to arrive. Among the first of them was Walter.

"Let's face it, Jack," Walter said as he stuffed an hors d'oeuvre in his mouth. "You're not gonna get video interest until you get out another book. And you're not going to get another book until you pay the publisher."

"Doesn't he pay me?" asked Jack. "I thought books were supposed to make money."

"For the publisher!" explained Walter firmly as he reached for another hors d'oeuvre and placed it whole in his mouth. "Now you have three speaking dates coming up: the eighteenth, Modesto, the Wall Applications Association . . ."

"Is that anything like wall*paper*?" asked Jack, already bored at the prospect.

"The twenty-first, Tampa, American Sand and Gravel Congress . . ." continued Walter.

"Didn't I do the Grit conference, like, two months ago?" Jack asked jokingly.

"Jack, these people are not interested in your jokes," said Walter, barely hiding his impatience. "Their focus is on expanding market share."

"Really?" Jack snapped back. "When are you gonna focus on getting me better jobs?"

"I got you one," Walter said proudly. "Investment Strategies of New Orleans, the twenty-fourth. Five grand! You get on the Other People's Money circuit, you won't have to work for industries like Wall Applications ever again!"

For the first time that evening Jack was impressed. "Really? A summit like that could lead to an infomercial."

"Keep your fingers crossed," said Walter. "And if I may say, I endorse your engagement to Celeste. Without family obligations you're vulnerable to drift."

Just then Jack spied Matthew, Celeste's seven-year-old nephew. The boy looked uncomfortable in a blazer and tie and was sitting by himself in the corner. "Excuse me," Jack told Walter. "I think I'll drift right now."

Jack walked straight over to Matthew and playfully grabbed him by the collar. "Step into my office," he said to Matthew, whose face lit up when he saw his future uncle.

Jack led Matthew into his old bedroom. The room was still filled with many of the things Jack had grown up with. There was an old Mets pennant on the wall, a Rolling Stones album cover, and posters of all kinds of old-time stars like Walt Frazier, Joe Namath, and W.C. Fields. But most of all there were shelves and shelves of beautifully hand-carved animals. The kind that Jack knew boys loved.

"Wow, these are old," said Matthew as he played with one of the carved statues.

"About as old as I am," said Jack.

"Wow."

"These are magic animals, Matt," said Jack. "My father made them when he was alive."

Just then the door burst open. Celeste stood there with a big smile and a handful of letters. "Time for telegrams!" she announced excitedly.

"Now?" asked Jack, feeling as if he were a little kid whose fun was being spoiled.

"Sure, now," said Celeste. Then she joked,: "Unless you don't want to get engaged."

"Oh, *I do I do I do I do*," replied Jack playfully. "See? I'm practicing for the wedding."

Celeste smiled warmly as she watched Matthew playing with Jack's old toys. "You're so great with kids," she said kissing Jack on his forehead.

"You can play with these animals as much as you want," Jack told Matthew as he followed Celeste out of the room.

"What?" he heard Matthew call from behind. "You don't have Nintendo?"

A few minutes later Jack was sitting in a chair with a stack of opened telegrams in his lap. So many people had sent their best wishes and it made Jack feel good.

"'*You've only just begun. A kiss for luck and you're on your way*,'" Jack read as he opened another telegram. "'*From Walter.*'"

"That's lovely," exclaimed a relative from across the room.

"It's from a song," Walter whispered to Jack.

Just then the doorbell rang. Another telegram had arrived. Jack's mother handed it to him.

"Here," she said. "We just got another one."

Jack opened it. "'*Dear Mr. Corcoran,*'" he read. "'*We regret to inform you of . . . the death . . . of your father . . .*'"

Some uncomfortable giggles were heard around the room.

"That's original, I guess," said Jack, thinking the telegram was some kind of joke. After all, he knew that his father had died before he was even born.

"I hope no one thought it was funny," said his mom.

"Wait a minute," said Jack, reading further. "This says he died a month ago in Maryland."

Jack's mother abruptly snatched the telegram away. "It's not funny at all," she said, clearly disturbed.

But Jack grabbed the telegram back and continued to read aloud: "'*We have been placed in charge of his effects and a rather large inheritance. We strongly recommend that you come to our offices as soon as possible to claim same. Trowbridge Bowers, Attorney at Law.'"*

A stunned silence filled the room.

3

Jack called Trowbridge Bowers the next morning. By that afternoon he was on a flight to the lawyer's office in Maryland, the telegram crumpled in his hand.

It was all so confusing. And as he sat on the plane he thought back to the conversation he had with his mother the night before. The engagement party was over and everyone had gone home. He, Celeste, and his mother were silently doing the dishes. Each one was avoiding bringing up the subject of the telegram.

"Mom," Jack finally said as he dried a casserole. "Mom, you can't just say, 'Okay, so maybe he hasn't been dead all those years, let's do the dishes.'"

"Well, what can I say," Jack's mom said as she scrubbed a frying pan.

"But you told me he died," insisted Jack. "Before I was born. Saving a little boy from drowning in icy water, he jumped in through the ice and — !"

Jack stopped himself. This was material he used for his motivational speeches. Now it all seemed like a pack of lies.

"Calm down, Jackie —" his mom said.

"I had a father all these years!" exclaimed Jack, "And I didn't know it! Now that I *do* know it, I *don't* have one! Am I crazy here, or what?"

Jack looked at Celeste, but she looked helpless, as if caught somewhere between him and his mother.

"I left him, Jack," his mother explained. "I left him and I took you with me and I didn't tell him where we were going."

Jack didn't understand. "Was he mean to you or something?" he asked.

"No, he wasn't mean to me."

"Was he a criminal? What?"

"He wasn't a criminal."

"Mom, tell me. *What was he?*"

Jack's mother paused. Then she handed him the clean frying pan and said, "He was irresponsible."

"Irresponsible?"

"He'd never hold down a job. He was always moving us from one place or another. We had no home. I couldn't count on a man like that when I had a baby."

"He was irresponsible, so you killed him," Jack said, trying to make sense of her deception.

"Oh, Jack. She didn't kill him," Celeste interrupted.

"She did!" insisted Jack. "She drowned him!" At least that's how it felt to Jack. Even if she hadn't really *drowned* his father, she'd made up the story. And it seemed real to him.

"I couldn't have him influencing you," Jack's mother tried to explain. "Boys learn from their fathers."

"Well," Jack said sharply. "I'll just have to take your word on that." And with that he turned on his heel and walked away.

"My name is Jack Corcoran," Jack said to a pretty receptionist as he entered the Trowbridge Bowers law office that afternoon. He pulled the telegram from his pocket and put it on her desk.

"You're him!" the receptionist said excitedly. Then she called out, "Mr. Bowers! It's the — son! The heir!"

Wow, Jack thought. There must be a pretty big inheritance if even the receptionist is excited.

A door to an inner office burst open and a nervous-looking little man emerged. Jack assumed he was Mr. Bowers. He seemed relieved to see Jack.

"Yes, well," Mr. Bowers said, taking Jack by the arm. "At last. Come in, Mr. Corcoran." Then he turned to his receptionist and said: "Have the — *you know* — brought around to the window."

The receptionist nodded and left.

Jack allowed the nervous Mr. Bowers to lead

him into the inner office. As he sat down in a chair he couldn't help feeling as if something very strange was going on.

"All right, sir," said Bowers as he pulled some papers out of a file cabinet. "Took a while to find you. I know this comes as a shock."

"Mr. Bowers," said Jack. "I never knew my father."

"Nor did I," said Bowers. "Heart attack. He happened to be — *er* — passing through town, and since I represent the — *er* — facility where he was appearing, it fell to me to take charge of the — *er* — effects . . ."

"'Appearing'?" asked Jack, confused.

"This should clarify," said Bowers. And with that he walked over and opened an old trunk. Then he pulled out an enormous two-foot-long red shoe and showed it to Jack.

"My father was a giant?" asked Jack.

"We saved his nose," said Bowers, who then reached into the trunk and pulled out a shiny red fake clown's nose.

"I had a clown for a dad?" Jack asked in astonishment.

"A very jolly one, I understand," said Bowers. "Traveled with a small circus. When he passed away the caravan moved on."

"My father the clown," muttered Jack. He was stunned by it all. Then, remembering his own motivational advice, he decided to *get over it.*

"I'm over it," he said. "How much am I inheriting?"

Mr. Bowers showed Jack the papers on his desk. "Right here is the amount," he said, pointing to a spot on one of the papers.

Jack's eyes popped open. "Thirty-five thousand dollars?" he asked gleefully. "Well! Thanks, Dad, for something! I can get out from behind with that kind of money. Do I have to sign something?"

"Yes," said Bowers. "Right here."

Jack signed the papers. As soon as he was done he noticed that Mr. Bowers let out a long sign of relief.

"Excuse me for asking," Mr. Bowers began, "but this is a great deal of money. How will you be paying the thirty-five thousand?"

Jack's mouth dropped open in shock. "What? Wait a minute. *Me* pay *you?*"

"Why, yes," replied Bowers. "Medical expenses, burial, my fee, property damages. And then there's the upkeep."

"Upkeep?" asked Jack. "Of a trunk?"

Just then a loud sound, like a blaring trumpet, came from outside. Mr. Bowers turned to the window and drew the curtains apart.

"There's your inheritance, Mr. Corcoran," said Mr. Bowers.

Jack nearly fell out of his chair. For standing on the other side of the window was a huge, twenty-five-foot-long elephant.

4

"**O**h, no! I don't want it!" exclaimed Jack once he saw the enormous creature his father had left him. "Why? Why would the man leave me an elephant?"

Suddenly Jack heard a loud *crunch*. The elephant had just crushed the fence outside Mr. Bowers's office.

"There's your damage," pointed Mr. Bowers. "It hates fences."

"Oh, no," said Jack. "I'm not paying for what that elephant does. You keep it. I'll take the trunk. My father never gave me enough toys."

"Mr. Corcoran, I'm not in the elephant business," said Mr. Bowers. "The elephant is legally yours."

Suddenly another loud *crash* came from outside. The elephant was wreaking havoc.

"I'm not responsible," said Jack. "I was misled. I'm out of here!" And with that he picked up his father's traveling trunk and left the office.

Jack had not gone half a block when he saw that his father's elephant had left a swath of destruction in its wake. Knocked over trash cans, bent parking meters, and overturned cars were everywhere.

"It's him! The elephant man!" a shopkeeper whose awning had been knocked down by the elephant shouted as Jack passed. Jack realized that they recognized his father's traveling trunk and assumed that he was the owner of the elephant. Soon the other townspeople were pointing their fingers at Jack. Before long a mob was chasing him down the street.

Jack turned a corner and ducked inside an alley. He waited until the mob had passed, feeling lucky that they had not caught him. From the angry looks on their faces he wasn't sure what they would have done to him if they *had* caught him. He felt he was too young to die.

Jack was about to leave the alley when he heard the sound of munching coming from behind him. He froze. Then he slowly turned his head. The elephant was standing directly behind him. And it was eating the fragrant contents of a large flowerbox.

All of a sudden the elephant stopped chewing. Jack could tell that it had seen him. He and the elephant locked eyes and for a long moment they stared at each other. Jack was certain it was his imagination, but he could swear the elephant was looking as though it *liked* him.

All at once the elephant began moving toward Jack, crushing a lawn chair as it did so.

Terrified, Jack took several steps backwards and then made a mad dash back toward the main street.

But no matter how fast Jack ran or how far he went, the elephant followed close behind, crushing and stomping anything that was in its path. Finally Jack ducked through an alleyway that was just too narrow for the huge elephant to squeeze through. He emerged on the other side and sighed with relief. The elephant was nowhere to be seen.

Jack looked around and noticed that he had stumbled into the town graveyard. All about him were gravestones. Exhausted from running, he placed his father's traveling trunk down and sat on it. He needed a rest.

So much had happened since he got the news of his father's death last night. He wasn't sure what he should do. Should he be mad at his mother for not telling him the truth? Maybe there was a good reason for why she lied to him. On the other hand, if she hadn't lied to him he may have been like the other kids when he was growing up. He may have had a father. Instead, all he got was an elephant.

It was at that very moment that Jack felt something thick and wet touch the back of his neck.

Jack jumped off the trunk and spun around. It was the elephant! And now it was heading right toward him.

Jack cowered, afraid that any moment he would be trampled by the huge thick-skinned, fan-eared creature with the long tusks. But after a moment Jack heard the elephant let out a long, mournful cry. He looked up. Instead of chasing him, the elephant had walked right by him. It was now standing by a gravestone, its huge eyes watering with sadness.

Jack had never seen an elephant cry before. In fact, he couldn't remember when he had seen an actual elephant before. He looked down at the gravestone at the elephant's feet and felt his own heart sink as he read the name on it:

KIRBY CORCORAN, 1932-1995

It was his father's grave. And the elephant was paying its last respects!

Just then a police car pulled up to the graveyard. Jack could see that Mr. Bowers was inside the car on the passenger side.

"If you don't take charge of this elephant you're going to jail," Mr. Bowers called out to Jack through the car window.

"You!" Jack said to Mr. Bowers in an accusing tone of voice. "You weasel-faced con man! I was defrauded! I have to make speeches in Modesto, Tampa, and New Orleans. And my apartment has a no-pets clause!"

"I'll slap a lien on that dwelling and garnish your fees for those speeches," threatened the lawyer. "And if you don't pay me thirty-five thousand dollars within fourteen days, you might as well pitch a tent in our little courtroom."

"You well-dressed worm!" shouted Jack. And with that, he attacked the door of the police car, trying to get at Mr. Bowers. That's when the policeman who was driving the car leaped out and pinned him against the hood with his billy club.

"Folks in this town used to think we hated New Yorkers more than anything," the policeman told Jack. "Now they run a close second to elephants. And you are an elephant-owning New Yorker who has assaulted a police car and slandered our most prominent attorney."

Just then Jack's phone beeped. The policeman reached into Jack's pocket and answered it. "It's your mommy," he told Jack, handing him the phone.

Jack took the phone. "I can't talk now," he told his mom. "You don't know him," he said, explaining who it was who answered the phone. "He's a new friend. I've got to go." Then he hung up and put the phone away.

Just then the elephant nudged its huge trunk in front of Jack and pushed the policeman away. Then it nuzzled its nose affectionately into Jack's face and neck.

"I believe your elephant likes you," said the policeman. "I believe you remind your elephant of your old man."

Jack sighed. He began to feel as if he would have to care for the elephant after all. "Didn't my father leave any instructions?" he asked Mr. Bowers.

Mr. Bowers opened the patrol car window and handed Jack a crumpled piece of notepaper. "Here's your father's will," he told Jack. "For what it's worth."

"Do you know the elephant's name?"

"Vera," replied Mr. Bowers.

Jack rolled his eyes. His father had named the elephant after his mother.

5

Jack waited in the graveyard and watched as Vera stood at his father's grave. It was a silly sight, Jack thought. An elephant standing at a grave. But there was something about the way Vera gently stroked her huge trunk against his father's gravestone that made Jack think maybe this elephant was something special.

"You miss him, huh?" Jack said to Vera. "Well, I've been missing him all my life." He unfolded the small piece of paper Mr. Bowers had given him. At the top, in shaky handwriting were the words LAST WILL AND TESTAMENT. Jack began to read from the paper:

"*I have a son Jackie,*'" he read. "*Somewhere in New York, last I hear. I will him everything. His mother probably listed as Vera Corcoran. To Jackie: I know I haven't been the best father. But do me a favor, son: Take care of her.'*"

Jack grimaced. It wasn't that his dad hadn't

been the *best* father, he thought. He hadn't been *any* father at all. And as far as taking care of Vera was concerned there were no instructions as to how that should be done. And he doubted that there were any books called *How to Care for Your New Pet Elephant.*

Jack noticed something else scribbled at the end of the will. "*If stuck, call Blockhead — K.C.,*'" he struggled to read. "Call Blockhead? What does that mean? Call Vera blockhead? Hey, Blockhead!"

Vera made a hurt-sounding grunt.

"Don't get huffy," Jack told the elephant. "That's dad's sole bit of advice."

Jack knew he had to think fast. He had to get rid of Vera and get back to his regular life. The only way to pay Mr. Bowers the thirty-five thousand dollars he owed him was to get back on the motivational speaking circuit in a big way. He decided that as soon as he dumped Vera off somewhere he'd call Walter and try to set up some more speaking engagements.

But where was a good place to dump an elephant? Of course, Jack realized. "The zoo!" he said as he pulled out his telephone and dialed Information.

No sooner had he dialed than a huge shadow fell over him. He looked up. It was Vera. And she didn't look happy.

"Back off, Blockhead," Jack told the elephant,

shaking the phone at her. He could tell she was upset that he was calling the zoo.

Instead of backing off Vera nimbly wrapped the tip of her trunk around Jack's phone and plucked it out of his hand.

"Very nice," said Jack. "Is that a trick he taught you? Now give me the phone. Come on, Blockhead!"

But when Jack reached for the phone Vera took a few steps back and swung the phone away from his grasp.

"This is not a game!" said Jack. He was beginning to get angry. "Come on now!"

Again Jack reached for the phone. And again Vera swung her trunk out of the way.

"Put down the phone!" Jack demanded. "Right now! Step on it!" And with that he threw his arms apart and let out a long, frustrated whistle.

Suddenly Vera dropped the phone to the ground. Then, she lifted her huge leg and stepped on the phone, crushing it flatter than a pancake.

Jack was stunned. "You did that on purpose," he said to Vera accusingly. "Now we're incommunicado. Well, you're not going to get off that easily. Let's go, Come on. Follow me. Alley-oop! Huggabugga! Move it, Blockhead!"

Jack picked up his father's traveling trunk and led Vera out of the graveyard. He needed to find a pay phone, but he knew he couldn't just casually stroll back to Main Street to find one. Not with

Vera by his side, anyway. Instead, he carefully maneuvered around the back streets until they reached the edge of town.

"Hey, it's the clown!" Jack suddenly heard a boy's voice shout from behind. When he turned around he saw that three boys were following him and Vera on bicycles.

"I saw your show!" exclaimed another boy with excitement.

"Not my show," insisted Jack.

"You're not the clown?" asked the third boy. He sounded disappointed.

"He was my father," explained Jack. "Hey, can you kids direct me to the local zoo?"

"You shoulda seen that clown get that elephant to do tricks," said the first boy. "Just with all different whistles."

Jack could tell that the boy had happy memories of seeing his father and Vera at the circus.

"Whistles?" asked Jack. That explained why Vera stepped on his phone. She thought he was giving her a command. He tried whistling to Vera again, but this time she ignored him.

The boys told Jack that the zoo was only a couple of miles away. They led him there on their bicycles. The owner of the zoo was a short man dressed in flashy clothes. His name was Wee St. Francis. He had named himself after the saint who was famous for caring for small stray animals. But when he saw how big Vera was he shook his head at Jack.

"I don't have any space here," said Wee St. Francis. "My 'mission' is small animals only."

It was getting late and Jack didn't know what to do with Vera. "Could you recommend a facility that could contain her for the night?" he asked the small zookeeper.

"Try the junkyard," said Wee St. Francis.

The junkyard was located about a mile from the zoo. The owner of the junkyard told Jack that it would be okay for him and Vera to spend the night there. It would only cost three hundred dollars. Jack had no choice. He paid the man the three hundred and found himself a comfortable spot in an old broken-down Buick.

After a few minutes, while Vera stood obediently by his side, Jack opened his father's traveling trunk to see what was inside. There were the big shoes and the clown nose. There was an outrageous-looking clown suit with big red buttons down its front.

There was also a small wooden animal sculpture just like the ones Jack had in his room back home. This one was of an elephant. Jack lingered over the small statue, stroking its smooth curves. He knew his father had carved it himself. In his mind he imagined what it would have been like if his father had carved the statue especially for him. But in his mind he also knew that it wasn't true. It reminded him of just how much he missed having a father in his life.

Jack reached into the trunk again and pulled out a book of maps. Notes were written in the margins of the pages. Jack realized that these maps showed the different routes his father must have taken to get around the country while traveling with a twenty-five-foot elephant. He decided to keep this map handy in case he had to use it himself.

Finally Jack pulled out a very long wooden stick that looked like a backscratcher. At the end of the stick was a carved, tusked elephant head. But no matter how hard he thought, he couldn't figure out what his father had used the stick for.

Suddenly an idea flashed into Jack's brain. He reached into his pocket and pulled the small piece of notepaper that was his father's will.

"'*Call Blockhead, K.C.,*'" Jack read aloud again. "Wait a minute. Maybe that's not the old man's initials."

Jack went to the pay phone near the junkyard owner's office and dialed his mother's number.

"Mom?" he asked. "Hi. Mom, did Kirby have a circus friend in K.C. called Blockhead? He did? Vernon Sawitsky, the Human Blockhead? In Kansas City? Thanks, Mom!"

Jack hung up and immediately dialed Information for Kansas City. Once armed with Vernon

Sawitsky's phone number he dialed. A woman, Mrs. Sawitsky, answered.

"May I speak to Mr. Sawitsky? It's urgent," Jack told Mrs. Sawitsky. But Vernon wasn't home. So he gave Mrs. Sawitsky the number of the junkyard and left a message for Vernon to call him back. When Mrs. Sawitsky asked Jack who he was he answered simply:

"Tell him it's Kirby Corcoran's . . . son."

6

Jack spent the rest of the afternoon calling as many zoos as he could find. None of the zookeepers were willing to take in a new elephant. Most of them recommended the same thing: that Jack should call the San Diego Zoo. There was someone there who specialized in homeless animals. San Diego was in California. And that was all the way across the country. At first Jack didn't want to call there. It soon became clear, however, that he had no choice.

"Mo Newman in elephants?" Jack asked after he called the San Diego number another zookeeper had given him.

"Yes?" a woman's voice replied.

"I've got an elephant all of a sudden," explained Jack, trying to sound as casual as possible. "And all the other zoos said talk to Mo in San Diego. Oh no! Put that down!" Jack had just noticed that Vera had picked up an old junked Volkswagen. He continued into the phone, "My name is Jack Corcoran. I have an elephant I inherited from my father, the clown. You know anyone who needs one?"

"I need an elephant myself," answered Mo.

"You do?"

"On the twenty-fourth of this month I'm sending a small herd of elephants to Sri Lanka," Mo explained. "It's a gene-pool experiment. Do you have a breeding-age female?"

"Female, must be," replied Jack. "Her name's Vera."

"Then look at the bottom of her foot," said Mo. "See if it's wrinkled."

"Bottom?" gasped Jack. "How do I do that without getting flattened?"

"If you don't know how to do that," said Mo, "you have no business with an elephant."

"I *don't* have any business with an elephant!" agreed Jack rather quickly. "Hold on."

Jack dropped the phone and approached Vera. Brushing her trunk to one side he spread his arms wide and whistled just as he had done when Vera crushed his cellular phone. On command Vera raised her foot just long enough for Jack to study it.

"She's got a very smooth foot," Jack told Mo when he returned to the phone.

"That means she's young enough to breed," said Mo. "Where are you?"

"In a junkyard in Maryland. I can give you directions."

"A junkyard!" exclaimed Mo. "Get her out of there!"

"There's no vacancy at Best Western," Jack said dryly.

"You bring her here and I'll pay you thirty-thousand dollars," offered Mo.

Jack's eyes opened wide at the offer. "You will?" he asked trying to hide his excitement. But he still needed more to pay Mr. Bowers. "How about thirty-*six* thousand?"

"I can't go that high."

"I can't go that *far*."

"Bring her by rail," said Mo.

"How do you make an elephant take a train?" asked Jack.

"You don't make an elephant do anything," Mo replied firmly. "Treat her with respect. Show her you care about her."

"Yeah, yeah," mumbled Jack. "What I want is specifics. Exactly how —"

"I can't teach you by phone," interrupted Mo. "Are you feeding her properly? She needs about two hundred pounds of fruit, vegetables, grains, hay, and twenty-five gallons of water a day."

"How about thirty-*four* thousand?" Jack tried again.

"The herd is leaving on the twenty-fourth," Mo

said flatly. "With or without her." And with that Jack heard the line go dead.

Jack hung up the phone and immediately pondered his problem. Okay: He had a twenty-five-foot-long elephant, a traveling trunk full of circus props, and in five days he had to be in Modesto to give another motivational seminar. No problem, he thought. He'd just switch into his Superman costume and fly Vera to San Diego while holding her in one hand.

Then he remembered: He wasn't Superman. He was just Jack. He had to take a train. And trains didn't sell cross-country passenger tickets to elephants.

Just then the phone rang. He answered it. It was Vernon Sawitsky, the Human Blockhead, calling from Kansas City. Jack quickly filled Vernon in on the passing of his father.

"I'm sorry to hear it," Vernon said sadly. "He raised Vera from a baby, you know."

"Yeah," said Jack. "Instead of raising me. Look, just tell me how to handle her."

"Couldn't begin to show you that on the phone, son," said Vernon. "Why don't you come see us in Kansas City?"

Jack quickly agreed. Kansas City was closer than San Diego. And the sooner he learned how to control Vera, the sooner he could get her off his hands.

Just then Jack heard a loud rumbling sound coming from behind him. He turned around and looked at Vera. She was standing perfectly still. Then the rumbling sound came again. This time Jack could swear he could feel the ground beneath him shake when the sound came. An earthquake in Maryland? It couldn't be. He took a few steps closer to Vera and listened. The sound came again. This time he realized that the sound had come from Vera's stomach.

His inheritance was hungry.

7

An elephant was hard enough to handle, thought Jack as he led Vera along the highway. But a *hungry* elephant would be impossible.

They came upon a roadside diner on the outskirts of town. Jack had to think quickly. There were two large trash cans standing at the side of the diner. He emptied them and then filled them with water from an outdoor spigot. When he was done he led Vera over to the cans.

"Why don't you have a drink before dinner?" he told her. And with that Vera happily began to drink the water out of the trash cans.

Jack went inside the diner and took a seat at the booth. He remembered that Mo said Vera needed to eat vegetables, lots of vegetables.

"How much is your salad bar?" he casually asked the waitress when she had come over to serve him.

"Four-dollars-and-ninety-five-cents," she told him.

"No," said Jack. "The *entire* salad bar. Every-thing on it, except the dressing. How much?"

"Thirty bucks," said the waitress, looking at Jack as if he were very weird.

Just then Vera appeared at the window next to the booth. The waitress nearly dropped her order pad when she saw the mammoth creature.

"Twenty bucks," Jack offered for the salad bar. "And I'll take a meat loaf sandwich. To go."

After Vera had eaten her fill Jack led her to the train station. He hoped getting her on the train to San Diego wouldn't be a problem and it wasn't. At least, it wasn't for the man in the ticket booth. For a few extra dollars the man gladly sold him a ticket for Vera.

Jack guided Vera to their departing train. A ramp led up into a boxcar, but Vera refused to climb it. Jack tried all kinds of whistles to get her into the car. He just couldn't seem to find the right one. With one whistle she walked sideways. With another she sat down. With yet another she danced the Charleston.

"Look, Vera," Jack finally said. He had run out of whistles. "Get into the nice car. There's hay, there's water. And I'll meet you in three days with all the respect and caring you could want."

He whistled again. This time Vera turned, lay down on her side, and played dead.

"Now what is this here?" a deep voice came

from up the track. Jack looked over and saw a very unhappy-looking train conductor.

"What does this here look like?" asked Jack. "This here is an elephant."

"Dead?" asked the conductor. "Not on my train."

"She's not dead," said Jack. "You can see that. She's just playing. By the way, what do you mean *'your train'*? Who are you?"

"Hurst," the conductor introduced himself. "I haven't approved this. You got permits? You got a license?"

"No," said Jack. "But I called and arranged —"

"You arranged with the local fella," interrupted Hurst. "You didn't arrange with the train. You didn't arrange with *me*."

"But —"

"You, with no permits, want me to take responsibility for a tipped-over elephant clear to San Diego?" And with that Hurst pulled out his wallet and opened it up. Jack got the idea quickly: It was going to cost him a pretty big bribe to get Vera on this train.

"Mr. Hurst," said Jack, trying to think of a way out of the bribe. He decided to employ one of the techniques from his motivational speeches. "Let's look at it this way. Let's take those negatives one by one. First, Vera is not going to stay tipped over —"

"So you say," said Mr. Hurst skeptically. "Every

39

state, there's laws, there's inspections. That means every state line, my job is on the line. I get terminated now, my pension's thirteen-five. I make it through retirement, it's twenty-eight. That's a differential of fourteen-five. Now you take that by a factor of, let's see . . ."

Mr. Hurst did some quick math on a slip of paper and showed it to Jack.

"Twenty-six hundred — !" Jack exclaimed in shock. He didn't have that kind of money.

"You got thirty seconds, friend," Hurst told Jack. "We're gonna roll. With your elephant or without him."

"*Her*," corrected Jack. "Look, I have six-hundred bucks cash."

"To San Diego?" asked Hurst with a laugh. "An elephant? Obviously uncontrollable?"

Jack threw Vera a whistle and motioned her to get up. She remained tipped over.

"Why didn't you learn how to manage her before you took her on the road?" Mr. Hurst asked.

"You can't just pick up something like that over the phone!" Jack insisted. "How about we go as far as Kansas City?"

Mr. Hurst thought for a moment. "All right," he finally said. "If the two of you hustle in there right now."

"I'm flying!" said Jack as he started up the plank into the boxcar. Then, as if she had understood every word that had been said between the two humans, Vera jumped up and followed.

"Looks like she likes you," Mr. Hurst told Jack as he started to close the huge boxcar door. "Keep this door near about closed, Colonel. Anybody sees you two and you'll be walking the tracks."

And with that he closed the door the rest of the way.

8

The train ride was bumpy and uncomfortable. For most of the trip Jack sat on a pile of hay and leaned against his father's traveling trunk. Vera stood the whole way, quietly munching on mouthfuls of the hay.

Although he was exhausted Jack was unable to sleep. He took the little carved elephant out of his pocket and stared at it. Thoughts of life without a father raced through his mind. All of a sudden he hated everything, particularly Vera. Then he looked up at the humongous creature who was happily stuffing her belly with hay. He tried to tell himself that he didn't like her, but somehow he knew it wasn't true. Vera was a hard gal not to like. No, he realized. It wasn't Vera he hated after all. It was her master he hated: his own father.

"*'He and Vera always went over big with the kids,'*" he said to Vera aloud, repeating the words Vernon Sawitsky had told him over the phone. "But I was his responsibility! Because of him I

"It's him! The elephant man!" No matter how fast Jack ran or how far he went, the elephant followed close behind, crushing and stomping anything that was in its path.

"My name is Jack Corcoran.
I have an elephant I inherited from my father,
the clown. You know anyone who needs one?"

"Look, Vera," Jack finally said. He had run out of whistles.
"Get into the nice car. There's hay, there's water.
And I'll meet you in three days with all the
respect and caring you could want."

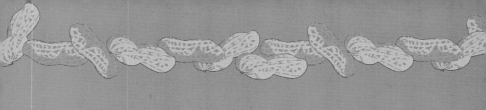

"I'm in a boxcar! Talking to an elephant!"

Jack and Vera arrive in Kansas City.

"I figure at this rate we'll be in Los Angeles
tomorrow night easy."

"I guess that's one of her tricks," Jack said.

"I don't know where we are. We're off Dad's map."

"We're never going to get to L.A.," groaned Jack in a cracked, half-crazed voice. "Need water . . . Why aren't you a camel? I don't want an elephant!"

Jack signaled to Vera, and she let
out a loud, happy trumpet.

was born in the hole. And I've always been in the hole. And now he's getting me in deeper. In the hole? I'm in a boxcar! Talking to an elephant!"

The following afternoon the train pulled into the Kansas City station. As soon as he led Vera out of the boxcar Jack found a pay phone and called Vernon Sawitsky. It wasn't long after that a large rickety red and yellow truck with what looked like a circus tent in back approached them. Across its side were the words SAWITSKY'S LITTLE BIG TOP: ANIMALS, CLOWNS, FREAKS OF ALL NATIONS.

The van came to a halt in front of Jack and Vera. The door opened and a boxy-shaped man in his sixties stepped out. Jack immediately noticed that Vera walked right over to the man and began sniffing him.

"Well, how you makin' out, Vera?" asked the man, giving Vera a hug around her trunk as he let her poke and sniff all about him. "That's a girl. That's the way they greet people," the man told Jack. "'Cause that's the way they greet each other. They'll check each other's feet to see where they've been. Don't worry, though, *I* just shake hands." The man took Jack's hand and shook it. "I'm Vernon Sawitsky, the Human Blockhead. I'd've known you for Kirby's boy anywhere, except Kirby prided himself on neatness."

Jack turned red-faced with embarrassment. Between being chased out of Maryland, spending one night in a junkyard, and another in a boxcar, he was pretty disheveled. Not only that, he smelled of elephant.

Vernon helped Jack load Vera and the traveling trunk into the back of his van. Then he drove them to his home in a suburb of Kansas City. Vernon's wife, Luluna, was there to greet them. Jack could tell right away that Vernon had met Luluna during his circus days. She was covered from neck to toes with tattoos.

After taking a quick shower Jack called Walter and reassured him that he would make it to Modesto in three days to give his speech to the Wall Applications' convention. Then, as he ate some sandwiches that Luluna had made for him, he leaned against the couch and yawned with exhaustion.

"You look beat," Luluna said. "Why don't you stay with us for a couple of days?"

"I have to get going," replied Jack.

"I don't want you to think all we eat is sandwiches," said Luluna.

"Anything you serve up, my love, goes down with a bang," said Vernon as he sat in his easy chair and ate his lunch. "And that's coming from a man who ate fire and swallowed steel." Then he turned to Jack and said: "Why do you think they used to call me the Human Blockhead? I used to put a spoon up one nostril and a fork up the other. Now that's something you don't often see!"

"Vernon," Luluna interrupted. "He doesn't want to hear shoptalk. He wants to hear about his father."

"No," Jack said firmly. "I'm not interested in him."

"Funny thing to say," began Vernon, "when you've carried his trunk all this way."

"Look, I just want to know how to deal with this elephant," Jack said, trying to change the subject. "And I'm kind of pressed for time."

"There he is," said Luluna. She was pointing to an old circus poster on the wall.

Jack got up and walked over to the wall. Across the top of the old poster were the words SAWITSKY'S LITTLE BIG TOP. Beneath the words were photos of all the acts in the circus. There were photos of a bearded lady and a lion tamer. There were also photos of Vernon, the Human Blockhead, and Luluna the Tattooed Lady.

Finally, in the lower right corner of the poster was a picture of a man in a clown suit sitting on top of an elephant. Jack knew that the clown was Kirby Corcoran, his father. And the elephant was Vera.

A lump filled Jack's throat as he tried to hold back the tears. It was the first picture of his father he had ever seen.

9

"My mother always said there were no pictures of him," said Jack. "That they were lost in a fire."

"Your dad didn't have Vera when he met your mother," explained Vernon as if reading Jack's mind. "They met in some town in New York State."

"Rockport," said Jack. "She was in college. She told me he saved a kid's life."

"Well, he was a fireman in the act," said Vernon. "A clown fireman. And they used to throw a baby doll around. Your mom traveled with us for a while. She took tickets."

"It looked like she was getting to be one of us," added Luluna.

"She had you," Vernon told Jack. "Then she was gone. She and you. Kirby left us for several years. Then there he was again. With Vera."

"I don't suppose he sat around reflecting upon what his wife and kid might be up to?" asked Jack hopefully.

"Well," Vernon hesitated. "You know your dad . . ."

Jack looked away, disappointed. The answer was definitely no.

"What Vernon means," Luluna interjected, "is that your dad wasn't one to open up much. He'd sit around carving wood."

"That I do know," said Jack as he reached into his pocket and touched the little carved elephant he had been carrying around since Maryland.

"Performing was where he let himself go," said Vernon. "Him and Vera were some team. Trained her himself. Don't know how he knew how to. I think they had a natural liking for each other since day one. Most amazing thing I ever saw. Old Kirby died doing what he loved. Wanna see my scrapbooks?"

"No," said Jack flatly. "No, thank you."

But no sooner had Jack said that than Vernon pulled out some scrapbooks from a shelf and opened them up in front of him.

"There he is!" exclaimed Luluna, pointing to a photograph of Kirby and Vera.

"Hey, what's he holding?" asked Jack. It looked like the backscratcher-type thing he had found in his father's trunk.

"That's the backscratcher," explained Vernon. "Vera responds to that."

"She does? I have it in the trunk!"

"Yeah? Show her that and she'll lead right along. That is, if you have the feel for her."

Jack pointed to another photo in the book. "What's that?" he asked. It was a picture of Vera standing on her hind legs pushing a large piano-like instrument fitted with steam whistles.

"That's the trick that made Vera famous," said Vernon. "Kirby would have her push our calliope uphill, all by herself."

"She always led the parade," added Luluna.

"World's only elephant to walk on her hind legs," said Vernon.

Jack was finding it too painful to look at these old pictures of his father. "Look, I really have to go," he insisted and headed out the front door. Vernon and Luluna followed him out.

"If you can just show me how to control Vera —?" Jack asked Vernon as he headed to Vera, who was standing patiently on the Sawitskys' front lawn.

"We were working the boardwalk in Jacksonville Beach, Florida," Vernon said, ignoring Jack. "And a lady came along the boardwalk pushing a kid in a wheelchair. The kid was born with a disease — what was it, Luluna?"

"Spina bifida," answered Vernon's wife.

Vernon continued, "And the kid wanted to play the games — throw balls at the bottles, rings at the pegs — and your father happened to notice.

And your father followed that wheelchair. And somehow or other, every game the kid played, he won. The wheelchair had teddy bears all over it. And the kid's mother noticed your father and she took him aside. And she said, 'Look, I don't know what you're doing, but I don't want any special favors for my son. I want him to earn things in life.' And your father said: 'You stay out of it, lady. You're not one of us. He is.'"

Jack was silent. The story had hit him hard. Up until now he had just seen his father as a bad man who deserted him when he was born. But upon hearing how Kirby Corcoran felt a special connection with a physically challenged kid, Jack was taken aback. Like the physically challenged boy, Jack's father must have felt different from other people, like an outsider. That must be why he felt so comfortable in the circus where most people are outsiders. Even Vera was an outsider.

Jack realized that he felt a little bit like an outsider himself.

10

Soon it was time for Jack to take Vera the rest of the way to San Diego. One thing that would make the journey easier, he realized, was if he knew how to control her.

Vernon remembered all the tricks that Jack's father had used to handle Vera. Standing on the Sawitzkys' front lawn, Jack watched as Vernon demonstrated how Vera responded to different kinds of whistles. Three tweets and she bowed. Two long tweets and a short one and she saluted. Four short tweets and she skipped.

"But I need to know the basics," said Jack. "You know: stop, go, get in the car."

"Simplicity itself," said Vernon. He whistled one tweet. "Go," he told Vera. Vera started walking. Then he whistled twice. "Stop," he commanded. Vera stopped. "See?" he said to Jack. "She's a pleasure. You've just got to develop a feel for each other. If she's sure *you* know what you want, she'll get it."

Jack tried the different whistles out on Vera. He was happy to see that they worked.

"What about the famous calliope trick?" Jack asked Vernon.

"She wouldn't do that trick for nobody but your father," said Vernon. "But I'll give it a try." And with that Vernon directed Vera to his van. Then he blew out a couple of long whistles and gave her a flourish with the backscratcher Jack had taken from his father's trunk. Just as in the scrapbook photograph Vera gave the van a nudge. But unlike in the photo, she wouldn't get up on her hind legs.

Jack frowned with disappointment.

"This trick must have died with your dad," said Vernon sadly. "So are you going to work up a show and take Vera on the road?"

"No," Jack said.

"What *is* your intention toward her?"

"Free her," replied Jack.

Vernon's mouth dropped open. "Do *what?*" he asked with surprise.

"Well, there's a woman at the San Diego Zoo taking elephants to Sri Lanka for a gene project," explained Jack.

"Sri Lanka!" exclaimed Luluna, who was standing nearby. "Who would Vera know there?"

"She'd have a real life," said Jack. "In the rain forest."

"Rain forest!" exclaimed Vernon angrily. "That's just another name for jungle! This is some kind of animal lib malarkey. Vera's not just an elephant. She's a trouper. Think of all the time your dad put into her. *And you want scientists to do research on her? Like she's some kind of wild animal?"*

"Don't get excited, Vernon," Luluna said, gently putting her hand on her husband's shoulder.

"She'll be with other elephants," insisted Jack. "She'll have babies. Also: I need the money. I'll get thirty-thousand dollars for her."

"Thirty-thousand dollars!" shouted Vernon. "Lemme tell you something, kid. People *insure* performing elephants for a million bucks!"

Jack's eyes popped open. "They do?" he asked eagerly.

"Sure," said Vernon. "That's considering future earnings. But, still, I know an outfit in Hollywood that'll pay you a whole lot more than thirty-thousand dollars for her. They provide animals for the movies. They'll make Vera a star. I tell you what we'll do: You need to appreciate your father's way of life more. I'll drive you out to Hollywood in my vehicle."

"Now, Vernon —" cautioned Luluna.

"Don't try to stop me, Luluna!" said Vernon. And with that he motioned to Jack to help him load Vera into his van.

"This is the life, kid!" exclaimed Vernon happily after they had been driving along the highway for nearly an hour. Vera was standing safely in the back chewing on some vegetables while Jack and Vernon rode up front in the cab. Vernon was acting as if he hadn't been this happy in years. And Jack knew why. Traveling the road with Vera was like old times for Vernon, the Human Blockhead. It was like being back in the circus again.

We'll put on a show along the way," Vernon continued with excitement. "You've got the clown suit, and the backscratcher, and I can still do fire! You know what your dad used to say? When you're not on the road, you're in a rut."

"I'm kind of a performer myself," Jack told Vernon. "I make motivational speeches."

"Airports and Hyatts and rent-a-cars, right?" interjected Vernon. "Naw! I mean the real road! Coming up with a way when there ain't no way. It's tough, but you're *moving*. You're not *stuck somewhere!*"

Just then Jack heard a strange clunking noise coming from under the hood of the van.

"Your father was a man who hated to feel stuck," said Vernon, apparently not hearing the strange noise. "He was a carny to the bone."

"So, who are these Hollywood people?" asked Jack. "Shouldn't I call them first?"

"Nah," replied Vernon. "We got to deal with these people face-to-face or they'll take us for rubes — *bumpkins* — suckers from the sticks. I'll do the negotiating. One time I traded a blind lion for a flatbed, ten dancing chickens, and a trampoline. See —"

Vernon was interrupted by the clunking noise from under the hood. The noise was getting louder.

"That noise," said Jack. "What is it?"

Vernon still acted as if he didn't hear the noise. "Our polar bear got arrested," he went on to say, "for breaking and entering. It wasn't really a polar bear per se — what we'd done was, we had taken a regular bear, and we'd bleached him."

Just then the clunking noise came again. This time it was joined by some smoke that shot out from under the hood. Jack heard a grinding sound, then felt a jolt. Suddenly the van coughed and came to a slow stop.

Vernon sighed and hit the steering wheel with his fist.

"Lately I haven't been able to get this old thing farther than the county line," he admitted.

Jack looked around. They had traveled too far to walk back to town and they were too far away to walk to the next one. They had stopped in the middle of nowhere. A human blockhead, an elephant, and him.

11

The idea struck Jack first. And no sooner had he pulled the backscratcher out than he could tell that Vernon understood what they had to do. In a matter of minutes they directed Vera to start pushing them along the shoulder of the highway to the nearest rest stop. Vernon found a phone booth and the three of them waited patiently until Luluna showed up in a station wagon.

"Last time you took off," Luluna said to Vernon as she stuck her head out of the car window, "you got three miles further."

Luluna told Jack that there was a truck rental yard eight miles ahead in the next town. Vernon handed him a business card with the name *Natural Talent — Terry Bonura* on it and a Hollywood telephone number.

"Just don't send Vera to the jungle," he told Jack as he got into the station wagon and sat next to his wife. "She never got along with monkeys."

"Who does?" asked Jack lightly.

"You know what else your dad always said?" asked Vernon. Jack shook his head. "Everywhere you go, every line of work, there's two kinds of people. There's carnies and there's rubes. Don't be on the rubes' side, kid. Don't live the life of a rube."

And with that Luluna turned on the ignition and both she and her husband drove off back to Kansas City.

Jack and Vera began the long walk to the next town. Jack carried his father's traveling trunk all the while. They stayed to the shoulder of the highway, but each time a car passed it slowed down to take a look at the peculiar couple.

It was very hot and Jack began to perspire. He took a handkerchief from his pocket and wiped his brow. When he was done Vera snatched the handkerchief with her trunk and wiped her brow, too.

Jack grunted. "I've got the wall application gala in three days," he said sourly. "How am I going to make that? What's the carny move here?" Vera waved the handkerchief back and forth. Jack thought she was almost mocking him.

"You better be worth a lot of money," he said to Vera. "That's a two-thousand-dollar gig! I've got to call Walter and make excuses. I hate that."

And with that Vera threw the handkerchief into the air. Jack, taking Vera's cue, leaped up and caught it. Jack smiled. He and Vera were making a pretty good team. He decided not to call Walter. After all, he realized, Walter was a rube.

The "Ugly Truckling" truck rental yard was a sight for Jack's sore eyes. His feet were tired from walking and his back was tired from carrying his father's trunk. Even Vera looked exhausted from the walk.

Jack immediately found the truckyard office and asked to rent a truck. The rental clerk's eyes nearly popped out of his head when he saw Vera. Jack had to make up a story that he had been transporting Vera across the country when his truck was hijacked by some crooks. With a suspicious look the rental clerk took the necessary rental papers out of a drawer.

In the meantime Vera caught sight of a food rack on the counter and slowly began to suck up bags of peanuts, crackers, and candy bars.

"Stay, Vera," Jack commanded, but Vera ignored him. Jack tried a few whistles, but Vera continued to eat the snacks.

"I need two credit cards," said the rental clerk as he arranged the papers on the counter. "And a trucker's license."

Jack handed over his credit cards, but he didn't have a trucker's license. "The hijackers took my trucker's license," he lied. "That's how these people work."

"No license, no truck," said the clerk.

"Do you really think I would be going through Kansas with a freaking elephant on foot?" Jack said, exploding.

Jack's temper tantrum worked. The clerk decided to rent him a truck without a license.

Jack followed the clerk to the yard and picked a truck with the words *Jack's Hauling* painted across its side.

"Here's one with my name written all over it," laughed Jack as he opened the back of the truck and led Vera inside. Then he went to the front, threw the trunk inside, and climbed into the cab.

"Seat's a little loose," said the clerk as Jack sat behind the big steering wheel.

"No problem," said Jack, faking confidence. Then he saw all the different kinds of knobs, gauges, and levers and nearly passed out. He had never driven a truck before and wasn't sure if he would be able to drive this one.

Jack turned on the truck's ignition. Gears ground. All at once the truck began to lurch back and forth. Jack was thrown forward. His foot kept hitting the accelerator. And all the while the loose seat kept sliding Jack farther and farther away from the steering wheel. Finally, Jack threw the truck into neutral. Then, finding a gear that felt right, he was able to ease the truck out of the yard and onto the highway.

Jack drove the truck along for about a mile before he felt the truck begin to ascend a hill. He quickly began to shift gears, but as he did so the truck seemed to lose speed. He tried several other gears, but each time he heard a horrible grinding noise. Something was going wrong. Soon the truck had slowed to a near stop and traffic was piling up behind.

Just then another truck pulled up beside Jack.

"Hey!" the driver shouted out his window. "Put it in first gear!" Then he demonstrated to Jack how to shift.

Red-faced with embarrassment, Jack did exactly what the other driver showed him. Now his truck settled into a slow, but steady speed.

"Ought to be a seat lever under your seat," the other driver added as soon as he saw that Jack was moving steadily. "Just don't hit the magic button." Then the driver pulled ahead of Jack and drove off.

Jack was able to drive the truck all the way to the crest of the hill. But no sooner had he gone over the crest than he started to speed up. Now he was going downhill — and *fast*.

Jack desperately tried to find the right gear for slowing down. He was being thrashed to and fro. Finally, his whole body was squished against the steering wheel and dashboard.

Jack reached down and frantically searched for the seat adjuster. Instead he found a funny-shaped lever. He pulled it, thinking it would help. Suddenly the whole cab tipped forward. He must have found the "magic button" the other driver had warned him about. Everything inside fell over Jack and he lost his grip on the steering wheel. He was now sitting with his feet over his head.

Jack reached up and grabbed a wire for support. He pulled the wire and the truck's loud diesel horn sounded. No matter how hard he pulled he couldn't turn the horn off. The truck was hurtling downhill. All Jack could see was the asphalt road whizzing by. He reached down and groped to find the stick shift. Then he yanked it and pulled it hoping to find a gear — *any gear.*

Soon the truck began to slow down. The hill leveled off. The truck finally came to a stop and Jack sighed with relief.

Now all he had to do was find a way to turn off that horn.

12

Jack stayed with the truck for a couple of hours before the state police showed up and arranged to have it hauled to the nearest truck stop. Next to the diner at the truck stop was a garage. A garage mechanic looked the truck over and told Jack the bad news: The truck wasn't going anywhere for at least two weeks.

Jack sighed with frustration. Why was it becoming so difficult to transport an elephant across the country? People did it every day, didn't they?

Jack led Vera to an outdoor water faucet and turned it on. While Vera drank, Jack reached into his pocket and pulled out the business card Vernon had given him earlier. He found a telephone and dialed.

"Natural Talent?" he asked when someone had answered. "May I speak with Terry Bonura? . . . Well, when will Terry be there? . . . Look, I have to make speeches in three days and I have a highly trained elephant. I've had several offers for her, but I thought I'd give you people a shot. I'm somewhere west of Kansas City with her. And I'm on foot."

The person on the other end thought Jack was joking and told him so. Jack became angry and insulted.

"I hope your superiors will appreciate your flipness," he snapped back and hung up the phone. He made a mental note to call back later and talk directly to the owner of Natural Talent.

Jack wearily dialed the San Diego Zoo and asked for Mo.

"Yeah?" came Mo's voice.

"Jack Corcoran. I've had a more attractive offer for my elephant," he lied.

"That so?" asked Mo. "Who from?"

"Terry Bonura at Natural Talent," replied Jack.

"I thought you might get hooked up with Terry," remarked Mo. "Terry wants to get hold of every available elephant. Do the right thing — get your elephant to the San Diego airport by eight P.M. on the twenty-fourth.

"This is not just an elephant," explained Jack. "She's highly trained."

"I don't care if she can play the banjo," said Mo. "Healthy and fertile is all I care about."

"Vera's a trouper," said Jack. "My father put a lot of himself into her and —"

"Yeah," interrupted Mo. "Your father was an elephant's best friend."

"You don't know anything about my father," Jack hissed. "He and Vera — Hello?" But Mo had hung up.

Jack sighed with frustration. He looked at Vera. She had finished drinking, so he pulled a candy bar out of his pocket and threw it to her. She caught it in mid-air and swallowed it whole.

Jack dialed the number for Natural Talent again. This time he got a number where the owner could be reached directly and dialed it.

"Is this Terry Bonura?" asked Jack.

"Whom do I have the pleasure?" came a woman's voice. She sounded very busy.

"I thought you were going to be a man," said Jack.

"And aren't you just crushed?" asked Terry playfully.

"No. I'm Jack Corcoran," said Jack. "And —"

"Aries, right?"

"No, Pisces. But, thanks," Jack said, blushing. "I have this elephant. It's trained and very talented. And Mo at the San Diego Zoo wants to take her to Sri Lanka. I was wondering what kind of dollar figure you'd pay. Mo offered thirty —"

"Well, *at least* forty," said Terry. "Listen, I'm in the middle of a movie shoot. Major motion picture. All animals. Mine. Call me back, okay? You sure you're not an Aries?"

Jack blushed again. It sounded as if Terry kind of liked him. He agreed to call her later and hung up. Then he went into the diner and ordered some coffee and scrambled eggs.

"Bacon, sausage, ham?" asked the waitress.

"Sausage," replied Jack.

"You know what you just ordered, don't you?" said a thin-looking man who was sitting next to Jack at the counter. He was eating a healthy-looking salad. "No nutritional value, whatsoever. Take me. All I eat is green. Green, green, green. Lettuce, kale, broccoli, spinach, parsley, celery. That's the way nature intended. Ever see a cow eat a sausage? Ever see a horse slop down a side of bacon? It's not natural! All that junk food is government waste!"

The man tapped his fingers on a cellular telephone that was sitting next to his salad plate. "As soon as this thing rings I'm picking up a load of bowling pins over here and hauling them things clear to Los Angeles. By the way, my name's Tip."

"Jack," Jack told Tip, looking down at the thin man's salad. Then he realized that Tip was a truck driver and an idea began to form in his mind.

"Then I'm redballing back this way with a load of avocados," Tip continued.

Jack took a quick look at the telephone number on Tip's phone. Then he excused himself and went to a pay phone and dialed the number. He watched as Tip answered his phone.

"Hello?" asked Tip.

"That bowling pin load," said Jack, putting on a fake voice. "We're going to have to cancel that. Termites."

"Termites!" Tip shouted angrily. "Like I don't know who's behind this? It's the government, right? Hello? Hello?" But Jack had already hung up.

"I don't believe this," Jack heard Tip say as he returned to the counter. "Now I got to deadhead clear to California." And with that Tip smashed his phone angrily against the counter. When he tried to make another call he realized he had just broken it.

Jack smiled. "Maybe I can help," he said innocently. And a few minutes later Tip agreed to transport Jack and Vera all the way to California.

13

By early the next morning they were passing through Colorado. The Rocky Mountains loomed across the horizon. Jack knew that Vera was safe in the back of Tip's truck and that most of his worries were over. He would shortly be in California. Then, after a couple of phone calls, Vera would be off his hands. He would be able to get back to his old life.

"The Rockies!" Tip exclaimed happily as he drove the truck. "Clean spring water, right? Wrong! The government don't want it clean!"

"Do you ever sleep?" Jack asked with a yawn. He had been listening to Tip complain about the government all night and had hardly been able to get any sleep at all.

"I slept last week," said Tip. "That's one of the benefits of eating all green. You have unlimited energy."

"I think I might spend some time in the back

with Vera," said Jack, looking for a way he could get some time away from the energetic truck driver. "She gets lonesome."

"Lonesome?" asked Tip. "Jack, it's an animal. Get ahold of yourself. Hey, by the way, I'd like to see some of her tricks."

Jack rolled his eyes. All he wanted was to get to California — and fast.

A few minutes later Tip pulled over to a rest area that overlooked a cliff.

"A check in with the main office," he said. Then he got out of the truck and dialed a pay phone.

Jack opened the back of the truck and led Vera out using the backscratcher to direct her. He walked her to the edge of the cliff. They both looked at the breathtaking vista with a panoramic view of the mountains.

"That must be Grand Junction," Jack told Vera. "I figure at this rate we'll be in L.A. by tomorrow night easy."

Just then Tip returned to them. He was holding a crowbar and shaking it at Jack. By the look on his face Jack could tell the thin trucker was angry. Jack realized the main office must have told Tip that the bowling pin shipment hadn't been canceled after all. Tip knew that Jack had tricked him into using the truck to transport Vera to L.A.

"Tip, get over it," Jack said as he stepped away from the enraged trucker.

"You don't do that to me!" Tip said angrily. "You don't do that to me!"

Tip swung the crowbar at Jack. Jack blocked it with the backscratcher.

"Tip, I had to do it," explained Jack. But Tip was too angry to listen to Jack's explanations. He kept lunging at Jack with his crowbar. Jack kept dodging him and using the backscratcher to thwart his blows.

Finally Tip took a wild swing that caught Jack by the suit coat. He pulled the suit coat down over Jack's arms. Now Jack was caught up in his coat and unable to defend himself with the backscratcher. When he looked up he saw Tip rushing at him with the crowbar. He closed his eyes, expecting the worst.

Suddenly Jack heard a frightening scream. He opened his eyes and saw that Vera had lifted Tip off the ground and was holding him upside down with her trunk. Tip had dropped the crowbar and was kicking and waving his arms.

"I guess that's one of her tricks," Jack told Tip as he adjusted his suit over his arms.

"I'm going to kill you!" swore Tip angrily.

Jack kicked the crowbar over the side of the cliff.

"The only reason you're doing this is I'm not popular with people," Tip told Jack. "There's nobody'd even do for me what that elephant did for you."

Jack suddenly realized that Tip was right. Vera had saved him from the mad trucker. "Don't make me feel bad about this," he told Tip.

"I hope you *do* feel bad," said Tip. He was still hanging upside down. "So, anyway: Does she do whatever you ask her to do?"

"She *never* does what I ask her to," Jack said, unable to take his surprised eyes off of Vera.

"She's not going to throw me off the side of the cliff," said Tip. "She don't have the character. And you're not going to steal my truck, either. That's grand larceny."

Jack frowned. It was true he needed Tip's truck to get Vera to California. But it was also true that he couldn't steal it.

Jack made Vera release Tip. The trucker fell to the ground with a loud thump.

"You hijacked me!" shouted Tip as he rubbed his sore bottom. "Your animal tried to kill me! And you're an interstate felon! I'll be back with the law!"

And with that Tip got into his truck, slammed the door, and drove off. Jack and Vera stood at the edge of the cliff as the truck faded into the distance.

They were alone again.

14

"**W**ell, we're on our own again," Jack told Vera. The elephant pushed her trunk gently into Jack's face. Jack responded by blowing into her trunk. Vera liked that and let out a long purr. Then Jack opened his father's map book.

"We better change course," said Jack. "Dad's got a southerly route here, backroads through Mexico."

Jack quickly plotted the course they would take to California. When he was done he opened his father's traveling trunk. Most of the junk inside was meaningless to him — except for one thing. He took out his father's clown suit and placed it on the ground together with the backscratcher and book of maps.

Then he hoisted the trunk and threw it over the side of the cliff.

Jack picked up the backscratcher, the map, and the clownsuit and tucked them under his arm. Then he spread his other arm wide. Vera responded by putting up her foot. Jack planted his foot on hers and allowed Vera to vault him onto her back. He sat astride her as if she were a horse.

Jack whistled for Vera to go, but she didn't move. He laughed, realizing that Vera was being playful with him.

"Quit kidding, you big lug," he told Vera. And with that Vera unexpectedly began to lumber forward and carry Jack back to the highway and down the road.

They rode like that for the rest of the day. By the time dusk fell Jack figured they had only traveled a few short miles. He realized that at that speed it would take them at least a week to get to California. Jack decided he needed another plan.

There was a large billboard posted on the side of the highway. Thinking quickly Jack hid Vera behind the billboard. Then he went back out to the road and held his thumb out as if he were a sole hitchhiker.

A small sports car stopped to pick Jack up. *Too small*, thought Jack. He waved the car away. Next, a large truck stopped for him. Jack waved Vera out from behind the billboard, but as soon as the truck driver saw the mammoth creature he stepped on the gas and pulled away posthaste.

Nobody, it seemed, was interested in a hitchhiking elephant. Jack and Vera had no choice but to keep walking. They walked until the sun slipped completely behind the mountains and dusk turned to night. But all that walking had made Jack tired. He looked for a place where he and Vera could spend the night.

A few miles off the highway was an empty field. Despite the darkness and the oncoming chill Jack decided to make camp there. Finding a grassy spot he lay down and wrapped his father's clownsuit around him to warm him from the cold.

No sooner had he snuggled inside the clownsuit than he felt a gentle nudge coming from above. It was Vera. She let out a long, pleased sigh. Jack knew she was happy. Happy because he was a Corcoran. And happy because he was dressed like a clown.

15

Jack and Vera awoke early the next morning and continued their journey. After checking his father's maps Jack decided to steer away from the main highway and cut across the lowlands due south. The terrain was dry and brown. There were no trees or plant life for miles around. It was a clear day and the bright sun beamed its heat relentlessly toward the earth. Jack and Vera had no water with them and they were becoming very tired and thirsty.

Not only that, Jack realized. They were also lost.

"I don't know where we are," he said to Vera as he checked his map. "We're way off Dad's map. And I'm due in Tampa day after tomorrow."

Jack and Vera trudged along. The desert sun became hotter and hotter as the day wore on. Soon Jack's mouth was dry and parched. Vera began to move very slowly and weakly. Behind them Jack could see nothing but endless desert. Ahead of them was the same.

"We're never going to get to L.A.," groaned Jack in a cracked, half-crazed voice. "This can't be happening . . . but I guess it is . . . need water . . . must have water . . ."

Then Jack heard Vera groan. "Yeah," he told her. "You want some water, too."

Then Jack heard something fluttering above him. He looked up and ducked. A large vulture came swooping down from the bright sky and landed right in front of them. Jack tried to scare the vulture away by shaking the backscratcher at it, but the bird was not impressed. Instead, it just stood there as Jack and Vera walked by and stared at them with hungry eyes.

"You carried back and forth across the country for years with him while I was stuck in Brooklyn," Jack said to Vera. "So get me out of this."

Vera let out a short toot.

"Will you speak *English* just once," Jack pleaded with the elephant.

Vera made another noise.

"That's no help," said Jack. "Why aren't you a camel? I don't want an elephant! Why don't you ever obey my whistles? Was Kirby so much more commanding? I wouldn't know. I had Mom and then Celeste. I got out of the house for one minute but now filthy birds will gnaw my bones. I want water! There's a log! Maybe it's hollow. Maybe it's got muddy water in it!"

Jack dropped to his knees and stuck his tongue against the short, sand-covered log he had spied, but the log was dry as a bone. He fell over onto his back, exhausted.

"Keep walking," he told Vera helplessly. "It's over for me. I didn't mean what I said about not wanting an elephant." All of a sudden Jack's mind went into a mad ramble of thoughts. "Why didn't Mom tell me it was the performing I loved, like my dad," he muttered. "Maybe I'd have been somebody instead of dying in the desert alone . . ."

Vera grunted.

"Right, Vera," agreed Jack. "Not alone."

Jack lay on the hot ground in silence. He was certain that he could go no further. That this was the end for both him and Vera. There would be no more hijacking of trucks or bribing railroad conductors. There would be no more attempts to get Vera to obey his whistles. There would be no more motivational speeches.

But just when Jack thought all was lost he felt a drop of water hit his cheek from above. Then another. And another. He opened his eyes. It had begun to rain.

"Rain!" Jack said, jumping up for joy. "Vera, rain!!!"

Jack and Vera embraced. Vera let out a long

happy trumpet. Soon the few scattered raindrops had turned into a light downfall and then a heavy downpour. Both Jack and Vera jumped around in the rain with deep pleasure.

"I'll never complain about anything again!" exclaimed Jack.

It was at that very moment that Jack saw a lone figure in a plastic poncho approach. When the figure got closer Jack could see that it was a man wearing a sheriff's badge.

The police! Jack thought fearfully. *Tip really did it! He sent the cops after me.*

16

Jack expected the worst. He held out his wrists and prepared to be handcuffed by the policeman. But instead of arresting Jack, the policeman led him and Vera a few miles farther south to a small Mexican village.

Jack realized that he had wandered so far off course that he had crossed the United States border and was now in Mexico. That meant he was safe from American law — for the time being at least.

The rainstorm had faded into a light drizzle by the time Jack and Vera entered the small village. The sheriff told Jack where the nearest restaurant was. He also told him of a stable where Jack could probably get Vera some food. Then the sheriff excused himself. He had more important duties to attend to. The rainstorm had left most of the village flooded. An adobe church, which stood at the center of a street, was surrounded by frantic people. The water had eaten away at the foundation of the church and it looked as if it might be close to toppling over. The sheriff joined the people and helped them lodge sandbags against the side of the church.

"Is help on the way?" Jack could hear a priest ask someone as he took a sandbag and placed it firmly at the base of a pillar.

"The phone lines are down," someone told the priest.

"There is no village without the church," Jack heard someone else say.

Just then a large cornerstone of the church broke away. Cracks began to appear along the walls and the bell tower looked as if it were about to separate from the building. A beam that had been propped up against the bell tower snapped in two. A statue of the Madonna was about to come tumbling down on top of the people below.

The villagers frantically tried throwing their weight against the bell tower. They pressed against it with their shoulders, palms, and backs. But the tower was too heavy. It leaned and separated from the building some more. The villagers cowered, expecting the structure to fall on top of them at any moment.

Jack wasted no time and directed Vera to the church wall. The villagers looked awed as they saw this huge creature lean its massive frame against the building. Many even crossed themselves and Jack realized they must have thought that Vera was a miracle sent from God.

Maybe she is, he thought to himself.

But even Vera's great strength was not enough to keep the church from falling. Her feet began to slip in the wet mud and the wall began to tilt again.

"Isn't there anything you can do, *señor?*" a boy asked Jack.

Jack thought quickly. He remembered the photograph of his father and Vera. The one where Vera got up on her hind legs and pushed the calliope. If he could get Vera up on her hind legs now, he realized, there might be a chance to save the church.

But then he recalled Vernon's words: *"That trick must have died with your dad . . ."*

Jack decided he had to give the trick a try. It was the only way to help the villagers.

"Vera!" he shouted. Then he whistled and made the high hand movements Vernon showed him back in Kansas City. Vera gave Jack a blank stare as the church wall slipped a little further.

Jack tried again. This time he moved his arms with larger motions. And when he whistled he whistled twice as loud. That was when Vera stepped back from the bell tower. Everyone's eyes were on her as she took a deep breath and heaved herself up onto her back legs. Then she pressed her huge front feet into the tower, preventing it from toppling over.

The villagers scrambled. They hoisted a few more beams against the tower and braced it from toppling any further. Smiles came over the villagers' faces as they thanked Jack. Some shook his hand. Some embraced him.

But Jack wasn't looking at the villagers. He was looking at Vera. His heart swelled with affection for the great animal. She had finally obeyed his command.

17

The next day the sun was shining brightly over the small Mexican village. The priests of the church had given Jack shelter for the night and fed him well. They did the same for Vera, too. Jack learned that the villagers considered him and Vera their saviors. They even put a sign outside the church that read:

SITE OF ELEPHANT MIRACLE.

Jack was just finishing his breakfast in the church refectory when a local artisan approached him.

"*Señor* Corcoran," said the man. "This is the plan for the shrine for Vera."

He spread out a large piece of paper in front of Jack. On it was a beautifully executed drawing of a monument that the villagers had planned to erect in Vera's honor.

"This is fantastic," said Jack with a smile. He wished his mother and Celeste could see him now.

"I can work from memory," said the artisan, "but I prefer Vera to pose for me for two hours every morning."

"That'd be great," Jack said as he glanced over at Vera who was in the yard bathing in a pool of water. "But, you know, I have to take Vera somewhere else."

"But she's the savior of our village," said the artisan. "We want her to stay. Her and you."

Jack paused. "I'm not sure where I belong anymore," he said thoughtfully. "But Vera has a calling. She's the elephant of my father and he charged me with getting her into the movies."

"And you will be in the movies with her?" the artisan asked Jack.

"With her? Me?"

"You are a performer, no?"

Jack beamed. If only his father could have heard that.

Jack excused himself from the table and went into an office where he dialed the telephone. After a moment Terry Bonura answered.

"You promised me you'd call," she said. "I waited and waited. I thought you dropped off the face of the earth."

"Vera and I were perfecting some of our tricks," Jack told Terry.

"I can't wait," said Terry. "We're shooting commercials till the end of this week at the L.A. Sports Arena downtown. I'll be the blonde with the tigers and bears. Oh, listen, Jack — one favor. Call Mo in San Diego and tell her you and I are definitely doing business together? She's called me twice now and I don't know how well you know Mo, but —"

"Consider it done," promised Jack. Then he hung up and called Mo at the San Diego Zoo. "Mo, I tried to let you down easy," he told her jokingly, "but I hear you've been harassing Terry."

"That would be like harassing a wolverine," said Mo bitingly.

"Just because she has a bigger budget and can afford more —" started Jack.

"So that's what it comes down to for you, huh?" interrupted Mo.

"To the contrary," replied Jack. "I'm not unsympathetic to this gene pool thing, whatever it is. But, you don't know Vera. I think she can do more for the elephant cause here at home than off in some backwater rain forest."

"You're trying to relive the past, Jack," Mo snapped back. "I'm thinking of Vera's future. You decide which is more important." And with that she hung up.

Jack hung up the phone and returned to the dining table. The artisan was now showing his designs to the priest.

"The movies will be Vera's shrine," the priest said to Jack. "How may we help?"

"The movie people are in downtown L.A.,"

replied Jack as he looked over his maps. "That's two state lines away. And I'm kind of —"

"Wanted?" finished the priest.

"Yes," replied Jack, only half joking. "Now I notice there's a reservation along here that overlaps Arizona . . ."

"We'll fix it for you," promised the priest.

It was like a scene from an old John Wayne cavalry movie, thought Jack as he mounted the horse the priest had brought from the stables. At daybreak the priest had given Jack some fresh clothes: a suede jacket with fringes, blue cavalry pants with a yellow stripe down their side, black boots, and a wide-brimmed white hat. He even strapped a sword to Jack's side.

Next, some of the villagers placed some garlands around Vera's legs and tied a big yellow ribbon around her neck. Then the priest and the villagers mounted horses and assembled in a single line. With Jack and Vera at the head of the line the priest led the orderly procession out of town and toward the red-hued horizon.

The procession snaked through the canyons of the southwestern countryside, slowly marching across the plains. That afternoon they reached a bluff. There they were greeted by a tribe of Navahos who lived on a reservation nearby. After hearing about how Jack and Vera saved the Mexican church, the leader of the tribe was more than happy to help them. He led Jack and Vera to the local railroad station. The conductor of the train was a Navaho as well and allowed Jack and Vera to ride on a flat car for free.

That night the entire Navaho tribe came out to see them off. As the train pulled out Jack waved good-bye to his new friends. Then he signaled to Vera and she let out a loud, happy trumpet.

18

By the time Jack reached Los Angeles he had made the decision. It was, he knew, the most important decision he had ever made in his life. Ever since he and Vera saved the Mexican church he realized that they were a team. Somehow he was continuing the legacy handed down by his father. Somehow, after all these years, he finally felt as if he had a father.

He decided he didn't want to go back home. He was going to stay and take care of Vera. What was good enough for his father was good enough for him. Now all he had to do was break the news to his mother and Celeste.

Jack found a telephone and dialed his mother's number. "Mom?" he asked when he heard her answer the phone. "I'm okay. Yeah. But, I'm missing the speech. There's something more to life than keeping a schedule and keeping house."

"Jack," his mother said, interrupting him. "I ran away and joined the circus all those years ago."

"I know you did," said Jack. "But why did you leave?"

"In a way, the story I told you was true," explained Jack's mother. "Kirby *was* always saving some kid from drowning. Giving himself away to strangers. It was up to me to save us. Somehow when I took you away I always thought he would try and find us."

Jack took a long look at Vera who was standing nearby playing with some street kids. "In the long run," said Jack, "he did find me."

Jack said good-bye to his mother. Then he called Celeste and told her that he was not coming home. In fact, he told her, the engagement was off.

"At least you could have had the decency to let your mother break it to me," said Celeste tearfully.

"Yeah?" asked Jack. "What would Mom have said?"

"That boys learn from their fathers," Celeste replied sharply. "Jack, is there someone else?"

Jack smiled. There *was* someone else, he thought to himself. Her name was Vera. But Celeste wouldn't understand that.

"No," Jack told Celeste. "That's why I'm calling you now, before my life gets too complicated."

"Well, I hope your mother and I can still be friends," replied Celeste, only half-joking. And with that she hung up.

Jack sighed with exhaustion. He felt both relieved and excited. The long trip was over and he had put his past behind him. After all these years he could finally start living his own life.

Jack blew a whistle to Vera and waved her over to him. Then he led her across the street to a large building. It was the Los Angeles Sports Arena. That was where Terry Bonura told him she would be.

19

The sports arena had been converted into a huge film studio. Trucks, cables, and cameras were everywhere. Production crews, makeup people, and camera people were busily working at their jobs. The arena was decorated to look like a three-ring circus. There was a brand-new automobile in each ring and Jack realized that the crew was preparing to film some kind of television commercial.

Animals of all kinds were everywhere, just as they might be in an actual circus. A bird wrangler was releasing a flurry of trained doves, a lion tamer was rehearsing with two ferocious-looking lions, a clown was even practicing pratfalls with a trained chimpanzee.

Jack saw a trailer and a large truck both with the words *Natural Talent* written across them. He led Vera over to them and asked an attractive-looking woman where Terry Bonura might be. The woman, who was dressed as a bareback rider and was grooming an elephant, smiled when she saw Jack. She told him that she was Terry.

"I bet I know who you are," she said to Jack once she saw Vera. "The big one is Vera and the little one is Jack. You look like you've been through the wringer."

"You just don't know," sighed Jack, thinking back on all the things he had gone through to get to Los Angeles.

Meanwhile, Vera had begun to smell the other elephant's feet.

"And this is Ginger," Terry said to Vera. "Vera meet Ginger. Ginger meet Vera."

The two elephants began to sniff each other hello.

"You look as good as you sound," Jack told Terry.

"Uh-oh," said Terry coyly. "This is trouble: Doing business with a man who knows what to say to a girl." Then Terry gave Vera an expert looking-over, checking her from head to toe. "Will she sit?"

Jack whistled and Vera sat down.

"You've got a way with her," said Terry. "You never wanted to put an act together yourself?"

"Funny you should say that," said Jack, who had been thinking just that ever since Mexico.

"Come into my parlor here," said Terry. She handed the elephants over to an assistant and led Jack into her private trailer. The trailer had been converted into an office. Photographs of animals covered the walls.

"We'll do Vera's deal first," she said once they were inside. "You may have your wife insured for a million dollars. That doesn't mean you can sell her for that."

"I don't have a wife," replied Jack. He saw that Terry seemed happy to hear that. "And I'm not asking for a million. But I owe a lawyer thirty-five thousand dollars. I had to blow off two two-thousand-dollar speeches. I had travel expenses. I'd have to get fifty just to break even."

"Fifty!" exclaimed Terry. "Jack, I do believe you want to take advantage of me."

"Terry, there are two kinds of people in the world. Carnies and rubes. And only a rube would walk out of here with less than he's invested."

It didn't take Terry long to decide. "Fifty it is," she told Jack. Then she put some papers in front of him. "Here are the papers. Let me find a pen."

Just then Jack saw a long metal instrument sheathed in rubber sticking out from under some papers on Terry's desk. It looked a lot like his backscratcher, but it was plugged into a battery charger.

"Hey, an *electric backscratcher!*" exclaimed Jack, picking it up.

"A backscratcher?" asked Terry. "Honey, that's an electric goad."

"A goad?"

91

"Don't tell me you got all the way here from Maryland without giving her a zing or two," said Terry with surprise. Just then the phone rang and Terry answered it. While she talked Jack happened to glance up and look through the trailer window. Terry's assistant was standing next to Ginger and Vera. He had an electric goad in his hand. Jack watched as the assistant yanked Ginger by the ear. When Ginger didn't move the assistant prepared to touch her with the goad.

The sight was sickening and it made Jack very angry. He decided right there that no one was going to do anything like that to Vera. He left Terry's trailer without even saying good-bye. Then he loaded Vera into the big truck that sat next to Terry's trailer. No one tried to stop Jack as he climbed behind the wheel of the truck. Everyone must have thought he worked for Terry. He turned on the ignition and drove the truck out of the arena and onto the highway that led to San Diego.

20

That evening Jack pulled the truck onto the San Diego Airport runway and up to a huge cargo plane.

"I got an elephant here for Sri Lanka," Jack told an airport guard. "The gene pool project."

"The what for what?" asked the guard, dumbfounded.

"This is approved," said Jack. "We're in a hurry."

"Nothing on the sheet about an elephant," said the guard, checking his clipboard.

"You just didn't get the word."

"The sheet is the word," insisted the guard.

"I'm not going to get this far and be stopped by you!" exclaimed Jack. But by then the guard had pulled his gun out of his holster.

"Turn this vehicle around now, sir," he ordered.

Jack had no choice. He turned the truck around and drove to the airport terminal. The terminal was busy with arriving and departing passengers,

93

many of whom were being helped by luggage-toting porters.

Jack jumped out of the truck, raced to the back, and unloaded Vera. Then he led her through the automatic doors of the terminal as if they were just a couple of passengers on their way to catch a plane. He led Vera straight to the security check-in point. Two security officers were passing metal detectors over passengers as they filed through.

"Got to catch a plane to Sri Lanka," Jack told the security officers. The officers' jaws dropped once they saw Vera.

"Just run the wand over her!" insisted Jack. "Quick!"

"You part of Mo's bunch?" one of the officers finally asked.

"Yes," said Jack.

"Mo's a character," said the other officer with a laugh. Then she ran the wand over Vera.

"The other elephants didn't have to come through here," said the other officer.

Jack realized the officers thought that Mo was pulling a practical joke on them. "I guess this one looked suspicious," joked Jack.

Once both Vera and Jack checked out okay the security officers let them through. Jack led Vera down the long terminal corridor and finally out onto the tarmac. The cargo plane hadn't left and this time Jack could see a woman with a clipboard standing in front of it.

He and Vera ran toward the plane.

"You Mo?" Jack asked when he reached the woman. He was almost out of breath.

"This Vera?" the woman replied.

Jack knew she was Mo. "We on time?" he asked.

Mo smiled. Jack sighed with relief. Then Vera gave Mo a sniff and began to purr. Vera must have liked what she smelled.

"Nice animal," said Mo. "Terry wouldn't meet your price? Because mine is still the same."

"Yeah," replied Jack. "Terry came up a little short."

"You're not kidding," said Mo knowingly.

"Where are the other elephants?" asked Jack, looking around the runway.

"In the plane. We better get Vera crated."

"Crated?" asked Jack with alarm. "Now wait a minute —"

"Cool it, animal lover," said Mo with a reassuring tone of voice.

Just then Vera began to purr very loudly. Suddenly her trunk began to vibrate and she lifted her ears up as if she would fly away with them. She looked right up at the plane.

"What's she doing?" Jack asked Mo.

"Exchanging ultrasonic elephant greetings with the other elephants inside the plane," explained Mo. "Too low for our ears."

Mo motioned to an assistant who then led Vera into a nearby shed. A moment later Vera came rolling out in an aluminum box that came up only to her knees. The assistant wheeled the cart to the plane.

"Each of the elephants flies in one of those," Mo explained to Jack. "They're patient animals. And they're company for one another. She'll be fine."

Jack walked over to Vera's crate. Vera leaned over and sniffed him all over. She seemed a little sad. Jack knew why: She was saying good-bye to him.

"It's okay, Vera," said Jack as he fought back tears. At that Vera extended her trunk to Jack. He knew what she wanted him to do and he gently blew into it. "Have a lot of little elephants," he whispered to her. "Your carny days are over."

And with that Vera started to rise above him, carried upward by a hydraulic lift that brought her level with the cargo door of the airplane. Then she was placed inside.

That was the last Jack saw of her.

"And my father would say I'm a rube," Jack said to Mo.

"Your dad wanted you to sell Vera to Terry?" Mo asked him. "So you're finally standing up to him after all these years."

"Only I had to squeeze all those years into twelve days."

Then Jack showed Mo the small carved elephant sculpture he had been carrying around in his pocket.

"This is nice work," said Mo.

"My father carved it," said Jack. "I want you to have it."

"Aw, no, you don't," said Mo, refusing the gift. "You're emotional and not thinking clearly. Elephants get a person that way."

"I guess they must," said Jack. He was still fighting back his tears. "Because right now I'm missing the biggest speech of my life, I'm fifteen thousand in the hole, I stole a truck, and no one's going to visit me in prison, because my fiancée and I have — *gotten over it*. And all I can think about is how much I'm going to miss her."

"Your fiancée?" asked Mo.

"No," Jack said, looking up at the plane.

Mo understood what Jack meant. He was going to miss Vera.

"They always say an elephant never forgets," she told Jack. "What they don't tell you is, you never forget an elephant."

And at that Jack blinked and finally let a tear roll down from his eyes.